Dedicated to Terue, whom I grew up with,
and her little ones, Waka & Kaho—SK

Special thanks to Michael Speier & Lydia Kwa.

Published in 2014 by Simply Read Books   www.simplyreadbooks.com
Text and Illustrations © 2014 Sleepless Kao

LIBRARY AND ARCHIVES CANADA CATALOGUING IN PUBLICATION

Sleepless Kao
        Duet / written and illustrated by Sleepless Kao.

ISBN 978-1-897476-76-5

        I. Title.

PS8637.L44D84 2011   jC813'.6   C2010-905680-9

We gratefully acknowledge for their financial support of our publishing
program the Canada Council for the Arts, the BC Arts Council, and the
Government of Canada through the Canada Book Fund (CBF).

Book design by Elisa Gutiérrez

Interior text set in Urge Text   ·   Title type set in Mandevilla
Manufactured in Malaysia   10 9 8 7 6 5 4 3 2 1

Sleepless Kao

Duet

simply read books

Ta-da!

Sora and Sarah
are always together.

They go for walks,
share favorite sweets
and the sweetest tunes.

Twin souls, friends forever.
"I know your mind, Sarah."

"I feel your feelings, Sora."
Every day there's something new.

Spring blossoms.
"Can you hear the song
inside the wind, Sarah?"
"I can, Sora."
"What do you hear?"

"Can you hear the whispers
of a little bird, Sarah?"

"I can, Sora."
"What is it whispering?"

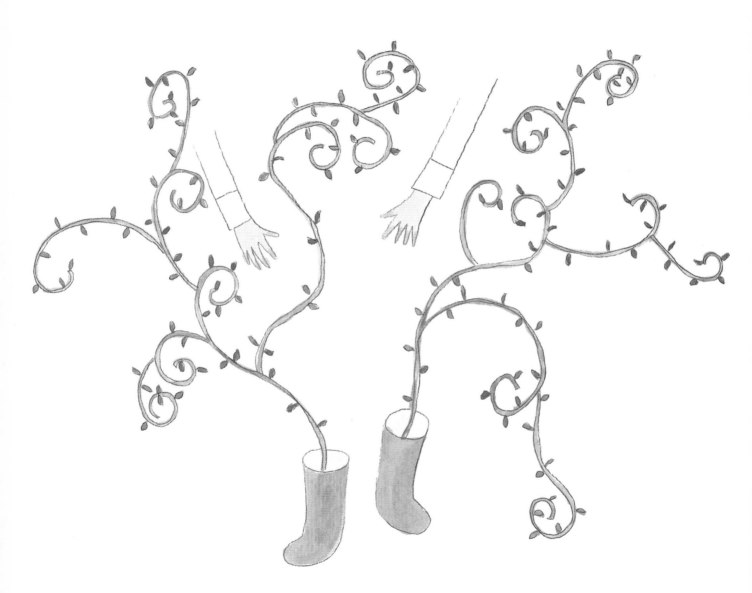

"Let's put soil and seeds
into our winter boots.
When shoots peek out
we'll have grown, too."

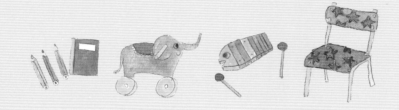

Sora gazes upwards.
"How tall will we grow?"
"I will grow as tall as you,"
says Sarah.

Summer shines.
Ice cream drips.
Sora gets a haircut,
short and fun.
Sarah's hair stays long
so Sora ties it up.

Autumn falls.
Time for school.

Sora goes.
Sarah stays.

Winter shivers.
Ding dong.
Ding dong.
Kay is here.

"Into the closet," says Sora.
"But I want to play with Kay,
too," says Sarah.

Sarah sits in blue darkness.

"Let's play dress-up," says Kay.
"No," says Sora.
"Let's play hide-and-seek," says Kay.
"No," says Sora, looking at the closet.

"Let's play with Tutu."
"Who's Tutu?"
"My secret friend."

"Can Sarah play, too?
She's my secret twin."

"Of course!" says Kay.

All together,
happy forever,
all morning long.

The End